Her Halloween Hero

A SMALL TOWN HOLIDAY SWEET ROMANCE

SWEPT AWAY IN BUTTERCUP BAY
BOOK ONE

MOLLY ARDEN

Molly Arden

Copyright © 2024 Molly Arden

All rights reserved.

No portion of this book may be reproduced in any form without permission from the publisher, except as permitted by U.S. copyright law.

Exceptions: Reviewers may quote brief passages for reviews.

This is a work of fiction. Names, characters, places, and incidents either are the product of the author's imagination or are used fictitiously. Any resemblance to actual persons, living or dead, events, or locales is entirely coincidental.

Contents

CHAPTER 1

Lily

THE AIR IS crisp and cool as I step out of my car and take in the sight of Buttercup Bay. The town is exactly how I remember it, nestled in the foothills of dense, vibrant forests that stretch out like a painter's canvas in every direction. Autumn has truly arrived here, and it's like stepping into a world where every corner is brushed with gold, amber, and crimson. The leaves crunch under my boots as I make my way toward the town square, and the scent of pine mingles with the sweetness of ripened apples from the nearby orchards.

This is where I spent so many of my childhood summers, running through these streets with my grandmother's hand guiding me, her laughter echoing through the cobblestone paths. The memories flood back, warm and bittersweet. But now, the Buttercup Inn is mine, and so is the responsibility that comes with it. I'm not just visiting anymore; I'm here to stay. The thought settles in my chest, heavy and a little overwhelming.

The town square is bustling with activity as preparations for the annual Halloween Bash are well underway. I watch volunteers string orange and purple lights between the old-fashioned lamp posts while others arrange pumpkins and hay bales into festive displays. Buttercup Bay has always taken Halloween seriously—probably because of my grandmother, Margaret. She practically invented the Bash, turning it into the biggest event of the year. Everyone looked forward to it, and she poured her heart into making it magical. The kind of magic that made people believe in the impossible, if only for one night.

I tug my sweater tighter around me, the rich burgundy wool blending perfectly with the autumn landscape. My auburn hair tumbles over my shoulders in loose waves, and I push a strand behind my ear as I walk through the square. I try to ignore the knot of anxiety that tightens in my stomach with every step. Can I really do this? Can I live up to the legacy my grandmother left behind?

She was everything to me after my parents died. I was only ten when their car went off the road during a storm. It's been nearly two decades, but the pain still sits quietly in the corners of my mind, occasionally whispering its reminders. Margaret took me in without a second thought, becoming my whole world. She taught me everything—how to bake pies, how to run the Buttercup Inn, and how to treat people with kindness and respect. But most of all, she taught me about this town, this community that she loved so fiercely. And now it's up to me to keep it all going.

I stop in front of the Buttercup Inn, its familiar wooden sign swinging gently in the breeze. It's a beautiful building, all weathered wood and ivy-covered stone, with windows that seem to glow even in the middle of the day. I spent so many nights curled up by the fire with a book while my grandmother hummed softly in the kitchen, the scent of cinnamon and apples filling the air. But now, the warmth I used to feel here has been replaced by a cold knot of doubt. Can I really live up to the expectations everyone has for me? The ones I have for myself?

I shake my head, trying to dispel the negative thoughts. There's no time for doubt. The Bash is only a week away, and there's still so much to do. I need to make sure everything is perfect, just the way Grandma would have wanted it. And that starts with the pumpkins.

I head inside the Inn and make my way to the kitchen, where Greg is waiting for me. He's already elbow-deep in flour, rolling out dough for what I assume will be one of his famous pies. The smell of butter and sugar greets me as I walk in, and I can't help but smile. Greg has always had a way of making everything feel a little bit better.

"Hey, stranger," he says, looking up with a grin. His sandy hair is tousled, as usual, giving him that effortlessly charming look and his bright blue eyes sparkle with mischief, reflecting a playful spirit that's hard to resist. "How's the pumpkin situation?"

I sigh, leaning against the counter. "Not great. My supplier canceled at the last minute. Something about a crop failure: I'm not sure what I'm going to do. The Halloween Bash needs those pumpkins."

Greg doesn't miss a beat, quickly dusting his hands off like he's just finished a secret project. He leans toward me, a conspiratorial smile spreading across his face. "Have you thought about asking Logan McAllister?"

My heart skips a beat at the name. "Logan McAllister? The guy who lives outside Buttercup Bay?" He's a reclusive mountain man, content to embrace the solitude of his rugged lifestyle, happily keeping to himself unless the necessity of restocking his pantry drives him into town for groceries.

Greg nods, his smile widening. "The one and only. I know he's a bit of a recluse, but I've heard his pumpkin carvings are out of this world. If anyone can help you, it's him."

I bite my lip, the anxiety returning. Logan McAllister is something of a legend in Maplewood Hollow. A man who lives in the mountains, rarely seen in town but known for his incredible woodworking skills. And apparently, his pumpkin carvings. But he's also known for being...well, not the most approachable person. The idea of asking him for help makes me nervous, but what choice do I have?

"Do you really think he'd help me?" I ask, consciously trying to keep the uncertainty from creeping into my voice.

Greg laughs, a sound that's both reassuring and teasing. "Of course he will. Just flash those big green eyes of yours and ask nicely. You're Margaret's granddaughter, after all. That means something around here."

I roll my eyes, though I can't help but smile. "It's not like that, Greg."

"Sure it's not," he says with a wink. "But seriously, Lily, you've got this. You're more like your grandmother than you think. Just go up there and ask him. What's the worst that could happen?"

I nod, feeling a little more confident thanks to Greg's encouragement. "You're right. I'll go see him tomorrow."

"Atta girl," Greg says, turning back to his dough. "And hey, while you're at it, bring back some pumpkins for me. I could use them for the pies."

I laugh, the sound ringing out and lifting some of the weight from my shoulders, if only for a moment. It feels good to let go, even briefly, of the worries that have been pressing down on me lately. "I'll see what I can do."

As I leave the kitchen, the knot of anxiety eases just a bit. Maybe Greg's right. Maybe I can do this. For my grandmother. For the town. For myself.

And maybe Logan McAllister isn't as intimidating as he seems. I guess I'll find out soon enough.

CHAPTER 2

Logan

THE WOODS ARE silent around me; the only sound is the steady rhythm of my chisel against the block of wood in my hands. The cabin, nestled deep within the dense forest, is my refuge—where the world can't reach me, and I don't have to face the memories that haunt me. The scent of pine and wood shavings fills the air, grounding me in the present, where the only thing that matters is the shape emerging from the wood beneath my hands.

This cabin has been my world for the past five years. It's small but well-built, with walls of rough-hewn logs that I cut myself. The furniture inside is all hand-carved—solid, functional pieces that reflect the hours of labor I've put into them. Each one is a testament to the solitude I've embraced since

Emily's death. The forest outside is thick and impenetrable; its silence is a comfort and a barrier that keeps the rest of the world at bay.

I pause, setting down the chisel and flexing my hand, the muscles stiff from hours of work. The late afternoon sun filters through the trees, casting long shadows across the cabin floor. It's a quiet life, but it's what I need. At least, that's what I've convinced myself. Out here, I don't have to deal with the pitying looks, the questions, the constant reminders of what I lost. The solitude suits me. Or at least, it did.

But lately, there's been an itch I can't scratch, a restlessness I can't quite shake. It's like a dull ache in the back of my mind, reminding me of what life used to be—of the love I once had and the dreams I once shared with Emily. We were supposed to get married, start a family, and build a life together. But all of that was taken from me in an instant, and the pain of that loss drove me here, to this cabin in the woods, where I could be alone with my grief.

I run a hand through my hair, pushing it back from my face. It's grown too long, falling into my eyes when I work, but I haven't bothered to cut it.

What's the point? There's no one to impress out here.

The man I was five years ago would barely recognize the man I am now—tall, broad-shouldered, with the kind of muscle that comes from years of relentless physical labor. My body has become a testament to the countless hours spent chopping wood, hauling supplies, and mastering the demanding tasks this isolated life requires. Each scar and callus tells a story of survival, a reminder of the strength I've had to summon to endure the solitude and the weight of my memories. My face is marked by a few faint scars from woodworking accidents, reminders of the countless hours I've spent carving and trying to lose myself in the work. The mirror in the bathroom shows a rugged, weathered face with blue eyes that have seen too much, eyes that have lost their warmth except in the rare moments when I can forget.

But today, something feels different. There's a tension in the air, a quiet unease I can't quite place. It's as if the forest itself is holding its breath, waiting for something to happen. I shake off the thought, chalking it up to my own restless mind, and turn back to the block of wood on the table. There's always more work to be done.

Just as I'm about to pick up the chisel again, there's a sound that doesn't belong—a soft, hesitant knock on the door. I freeze, the chisel halfway to the wood. No one ever comes out here. The locals know better than to bother me, and that's the way I like it. So who could it be?

Cautiously, I set down the chisel and walk to the door, every instinct telling me to ignore it, to pretend I'm not home. But the knock comes again, a little firmer this time, and something—curiosity, maybe, or that damned restlessness—makes me reach for the door handle.

When I open the door, I'm not prepared for what I see. Standing on my porch, looking small and slightly out of place against the backdrop of the woods, is a woman. She's in her late twenties, with auburn hair that catches the light of the setting sun, tumbling in loose waves over her shoulders. Her green eyes are wide and a little anxious, but there's a determination in them that catches me off guard. She's dressed for the season in a cozy sweater the color of autumn leaves and boots that are practical yet stylish. Everything about her speaks of warmth, life, and everything I've been avoiding.

And then she smiles—just a small, tentative curve of her lips—and I feel something in my chest tighten. It's a feeling I haven't had in years, something I thought I'd buried along with Emily. But here it is, rising without warning, catching me off guard.

"Hi," she says, her voice soft but steady. "You're Logan McAllister, right?"

I nod, still trying to process what she's doing here. "That's me. What do you need?"

She hesitates, glancing around the room as if weighing her options, second-guessing her decision to come here. The flicker of uncertainty in her eyes momentarily holds my breath captive, and for a heartbeat, I think she's going to turn on her heel and leave. But then, with a deep breath, she straightens her shoulders, rallying her courage, and meets my gaze head-on, a silent determination radiating from her. "I'm Lily Thompson. I... I'm taking over the Buttercup Inn, and I need some help."

The Buttercup Inn. That explains a lot. She must be Margaret Thompson's granddaughter. I remember hearing that she'd come back to take over after her grandmother passed away, but I didn't think much of it at the time. The inn is the heart of Buttercup Bay, always bustling with activity, and I've made it a point to stay far away from it. Too many people, too many reminders of what I've lost.

"What kind of help?" I ask, keeping my voice even, though the sight of her, standing there with her mix of determination and vulnerability, is starting to chip away at the walls I've built around myself.

"It's for the Halloween Bash," she explains, her voice gaining a little more confidence. "I was supposed to get a delivery of pumpkins, but my supplier fell through at the last minute. Greg Harper—you probably know him—suggested I come to see you. He said you're the best at carving pumpkins."

The Halloween Bash. Of course. It's the biggest event of the year, and I've always done my best to avoid it. But now, looking at Lily, I find myself hesitating. Part of me wants to say no, to send her away and retreat into my solitude. But another part

—a part I've been ignoring for too long—wants to say yes. There's something about her that makes me want to help, to step out of the shadows I've been living in and... what? Rejoin the world?

It's a dangerous thought, one that could lead to nothing but more pain. But as I stand there, looking into her green eyes, I know I'm going to do it anyway.

"Alright," I say, and I'm taken aback by how easily the word slips from my lips, almost as if it had been waiting for this moment. "I'll help." The decision feels both liberating and daunting, a thin thread connecting me to a world I've been so reluctant to engage with.

She blinks, as if she wasn't expecting me to agree so quickly. "You will?"

I nod, feeling that tightness in my chest ease just a little. "Yeah. I'll carve the pumpkins. You can pick them up in a few days."

The relief on her face is unmistakable, a radiant shift that brightens her features, and she finally lets out a breath she's been holding as if the weight of the world has lifted from her shoulders. "Thank you, Logan. I really appreciate it."

I give a short nod, not trusting myself to say anything more. This is already more than I bargained for, and I need a moment to process it all. She seems to sense that because she doesn't linger. With a grateful smile, she says goodbye and turns to leave, her footsteps soft against the wooden porch.

I watch her go, the spark she ignited in me still flickering in the quiet of the cabin. As the sound of her footsteps fades into the distance, I close the door with a gentle click and lean against it, feeling the cool wood press against my back. My mind races with thoughts and emotions, each one tumbling over the other like leaves caught in a brisk autumn wind. What have I just agreed to? And why does it feel like the first real decision I've made in years?

The cabin is silent again, a familiar stillness that has always brought me comfort. Yet, for the first time, the silence feels... different. It wraps around me not as a warm embrace, but as a heavy cloak, filled with unspoken words and lingering possibilities. The air seems charged, as if the very walls are holding their breath, waiting for something to break the spell of solitude that has enveloped this place for so long. It's not as comforting as it once was.

I push away from the door and walk back to the workbench, picking up the chisel with a hand that feels less steady than before. I stare at the block of wood in front of me, but my thoughts are elsewhere—on Lily Thompson, and the strange, unexpected warmth she brought with her.

I don't know what's going to happen next. But as I start carving, I can't shake the feeling that something has changed, something that might just pull me out of this self-imposed isolation and back into the world I thought I'd left behind.

CHAPTER 3

Lily

THE BUTTERCUP INN is exactly as I remember it—charming, cozy, and filled with the warm, inviting scent of cinnamon mingling with freshly baked apple pie. It's like stepping back into my childhood, where every corner holds a memory of my grandmother. The floors creak beneath my feet as I walk through the front hall, and I can almost hear her voice, warm and welcoming, greeting the guests who used to flock here for her famous pies and warm hospitality.

The Inn has always been the heart of Buttercup Bay, and it's easy to see why. The walls are lined with old photographs—black-and-white snapshots of my grandmother with the townspeople, celebrating holidays and milestones. There's a picture of her, young and vibrant, standing proudly in front of the Inn with a smile that could light up the whole town. She was the kind of person everyone loved, the kind of person who made a difference just by being herself. And now, all of this —this history, this legacy—is in my hands.

I step into the kitchen, the heart of the Inn, and the comforting aroma of baking envelops me like a warm embrace. This was where my grandmother spent most of her time, teaching me how to roll dough, mix spices, and bake pies that would bring people together. The kitchen hasn't changed much —there's the same old wooden table in the center, the same copper pots hanging from the rack above the stove, and the same worn recipe cards tucked into a box by the window. I run my fingers over the surface of the table, remembering how she used to knead dough with a strength and grace that seemed effortless.

But today, instead of feeling comforted, I'm filled with a strange mix of emotions. There's a sense of hope—renewed by my meeting with Logan—but also a nagging fear that I'm in over my head. The connection I felt with him was unexpected, almost startling in its intensity. I can't quite shake the image of him standing in the doorway of his cabin, looking at me with those blue eyes as if he could see right through me. His ruggedness intrigued me, and I was drawn to him in a way I didn't anticipate. But now, I wonder if I've asked too much of him. What if he regrets agreeing to help? What if I've put him in an uncomfortable position?

I sigh, feeling the weight of my responsibilities pressing down on me again. The Bash is just around the corner, and there's still much to do. I can't afford to let my doubts get the better of me. I need to focus, channel the determination that my grandmother always had, and make this event a success. For her, for the town, and for myself.

As if on cue, Greg saunters into the kitchen, his perpetual smile instantly lighting up his face like the sun breaking through a cloudy sky. He's tall and lean, with sandy hair that's always a bit tousled, as though he's just rolled out of bed and doesn't care to smooth it down. His bright blue eyes twinkle with mischief, sparkling with a playful energy that makes it impossible not to feel uplifted in his presence. He's been my rock since I returned to Buttercup Bay, always ready with a joke or a supportive word, and I don't know what I'd do without him.

"Hey, Lily," he says warmly, reaching for a shiny red apple from the bowl on the counter, its surface glistening under the kitchen lights. He takes a hearty bite, the crisp sound echoing in the otherwise quiet room. "You look deep in thought. Everything okay?" His tone is laced with genuine concern, a reminder of the unwavering support he always offers.

I nod, trying to shake off my worries. "Yeah, I'm just thinking about everything we still need to do for the Halloween Bash. And... well, I went to see Logan McAllister today."

Greg raises an eyebrow, his smile widening. "Oh? How'd that go?"

I feel my cheeks warm with a slight flush, and I instinctively look down, redirecting my attention to the apple pie I'm about to place in the oven. The sweet aroma of cinnamon and baked apples wafts through the kitchen, further heightening my anticipation. "It went... well, I think. He agreed to help with the pumpkins."

Greg chuckles, clearly amused. "That's great news! But why do I get the feeling there's more to this story?"

I roll my eyes, but a smile tugs at the corners of my lips despite my efforts to suppress it. Greg knows me too well; his teasing instincts honed from years of friendship. It's both annoying and endearing how he can read me like an open book. "It's just... I don't know. I wasn't expecting to feel such a connection with him. He's... different."

"Different, huh?" Greg says, leaning against the counter with a knowing look. "Different good or different bad?"

"Good," I admit, finally looking up at him. "But I'm also worried. What if I'm asking too much? What if he regrets agreeing to help?"

Greg waves a hand dismissively. "You worry too much, Lily. From what I've heard, Logan doesn't do anything he doesn't want to do. If he agreed to help, it's because he wants to. And honestly, I think it's great. The Bash is going to be amazing with his help."

I nod, feeling a little more reassured as warmth spreads through me. Greg has a way of making everything seem simpler and more manageable. His calm demeanor is like an anchor in the storm of my thoughts, reminding me that not everything has to feel so overwhelming. "I hope you're right."

"Of course I'm right," he says with a grin. "And speaking of the Bash, I've been thinking—we should add a Spooky Storytelling Corner this year. You know, something to keep the kids entertained while the adults enjoy the Pumpkin Pie Contest."

"That's a great idea," I say, the gears in my mind already turning. "We could have it near the bonfire, with someone telling ghost stories."

"Exactly," Greg says, looking pleased. "And who better to tell those stories than Logan? I bet he's got some great ones up his sleeve."

I pause, considering it carefully. Logan, with his deep, resonant voice that can capture an audience's attention, coupled with the alluring mystery that seems to swirl around him, would be perfect for that role. The thought of involving him even more in the Bash fills me with excitement, though it also stirs a hint of nervousness within me. What if he perceives my enthusiasm as pushing too hard? The last thing I want is to make him uncomfortable or feel obligated.

"Do you think he'd be up for it?" I ask, glancing at Greg.

"I think you should ask him," Greg says, finishing his apple and tossing the core into the trash. "The worst he can do is say no. But something tells me he won't."

I chew on my lip, feeling that familiar mix of nerves and excitement fluttering within me once more. I can't deny the magnetic pull I feel toward Logan; there's something about him that captivates me. But I'm left wondering if it's merely admiration for his undeniable skill or if it runs deeper than that. Whatever it is, a sense of urgency washes over me—I know I need to see him again and invite him to collaborate on more aspects of the Halloween Bash. It feels like the right course of action, even if it means stepping a little further out of my comfort zone, and pushing past the boundaries I've carefully constructed around myself.

"I'll go see him again tomorrow," I say, my decision made.

"Atta girl," Greg says, clapping me on the shoulder. "And hey, if you need a taste tester for those pies, you know where to find me."

I laugh, feeling the tension in my shoulders ease. "Thanks, Greg. I'll keep that in mind."

As Greg leaves the kitchen, I turn my attention back to the pie, the warmth of the oven seeping into the room as I slide it in. I close my eyes, letting it wash over me. This is where I feel closest to my grandmother, where I feel her presence guiding me, just as it always did. I can almost hear her voice telling me that I'm doing fine and that I'm on the right track.

And maybe I am. Maybe this Halloween Bash will be a success. Maybe I'll prove to myself—and everyone else—that I'm capable of carrying on her legacy. And maybe, just maybe, I'll find something —or someone—that makes it all worth it.

The thought of Logan crosses my mind again, unbidden. There's something about him, something that makes me want to know more, to see where this unexpected connection might lead. Tomorrow, I'll go back to his cabin and ask him to be a part of the Storytelling Corner.

But for now, I focus on the pie, on the comfort of the kitchen, and on the sense of hope that, despite everything, refuses to let go.

CHAPTER 4

Logan

THE RHYTHM of the chisel against the pumpkin is steady and soothing, each precise movement cutting away the outer layer to reveal the design underneath. This is where I find peace—in the familiar motions of carving, in the way my hands know exactly what to do without needing to think too hard. It's just me, the tools, and the pumpkin in front of me. Nothing else matters. At least, that's what I tell myself.

But as much as I try to lose myself in the work, my thoughts keep drifting back to Lily. It's surprising, really, how much I enjoy thinking about her. That spark I felt when she showed up at my cabin has been flickering ever since, refusing to go out. There's a warmth in my chest that I haven't felt in years, and it's unsettling. I should be focused on the task at hand, but instead, I'm replaying our conversation, the way she looked at me with those bright green eyes, her determination to make the Halloween Bash a success. She's got a fire in her, that's for sure.

And yet, with that warmth comes something else—fear. The memory of Emily is never far away, lurking in the corners of my mind, reminding me of what happened the last time I allowed myself to love someone. I can still see her, hear her laugh, and feel the way she used to curl up next to me on cold nights, talking about the future we were supposed to have together. And then, in an instant, it was all gone. The pain of losing her was more than I could bear, and it drove me into this isolation, where I thought I could keep myself safe from ever feeling that kind of pain again.

I run my thumb along the edge of the pumpkin, smoothing out a rough spot. The design is coming together—a cluster of autumn leaves intertwined with vines, intricate and delicate. It's the kind of work that requires focus, patience, and a steady hand. It's the kind of work that used to bring me solace, but now... Now, I'm doing it for Lily. And I don't fully understand why.

Maybe it's because she reminds me of Emily in some ways. Not in the way she looks or acts but in the way she carries herself, with that same mix of strength and vulnerability. Or maybe it's because I see something in her that I recognize—a determination to prove herself, to live up to the expectations of the people around her. I don't know. All I know is that she's gotten under my skin, and I can't seem to shake it.

I pause, setting the chisel down and flexing my hand. The workshop is quiet; the only sound is the faint rustle of leaves outside. The light filtering through the small window casts long shadows across the room, giving everything a golden glow. This place, my sanctuary, is filled with the scent of wood shavings and the faint tang of pumpkin flesh. It's comforting in its own way, a reminder of the life I've built for myself out here, away from the world. But now, it feels different. The solitude that once brought me peace now feels... incomplete.

Before I can dwell too much on that thought, I hear the sound of footsteps approaching the cabin. My heart skips a beat, and I know it's her. Lily. I've been expecting her, but the anticipation that comes with seeing her again is something I'm not used to. I'm both pleased and anxious, a mix of emotions that I'm not sure how to handle. I wipe my hands on a rag and turn toward the door, just as she knocks.

"Come in," I call out, trying to keep my voice steady.

The door creaks open, and there she is, standing in the doorway with a smile that immediately warms the room. She's wearing a simple, deep-green sweater that brings out the color of her eyes, and her auburn hair is loose, framing her face in soft waves. There's a lightness to her, an energy that contrasts sharply with the stillness of the cabin. It's like she's bringing the outside world in with her, whether I'm ready for it or not.

"Hi, Logan," she says, stepping inside and closing the door behind her. "I hope I'm not interrupting."

"Not at all," I say, though my heart is racing in a way that suggests otherwise. "Just working on the pumpkins."

She glances around the workshop, her eyes landing on the half-finished pumpkins scattered across the workbench. "Wow, these are incredible. You weren't kidding when you said you were good at this."

I can't help but smile at her compliment, though I try to downplay it. "It's just something I've been doing for a long time."

"Well, you're amazing at it," she says, stepping closer to the workbench to get a better look. "These are going to be the highlight of the Bash. Everyone's going to love them."

There's genuine admiration in her voice, and it stirs something in me—something that feels dangerously close to pride. It's been a long time since I cared about what anyone thought of my work. But hearing Lily say it, seeing the appreciation in her eyes, makes me want to do even better. Not just for the Bash, but for her.

"So," I say, trying to focus on the task at hand. "What brings you by?"

She hesitates, just for a moment, before meeting my gaze. "I wanted to check on your progress, of course, but also... I had an idea. Greg and I were brainstorming, and we thought it would be great to add a Spooky Storytelling Corner to the Bash. You know, something for the kids while the adults are busy with the Pumpkin Pie Contest."

"Sounds like a good idea," I say, wondering where this is going.

Lily bites her lip, a nervous habit that I find oddly endearing. There's something about the way her hair catches the light as she shifts her weight from one foot to the other, a subtle tension in her posture that makes her seem both uncertain and charmingly vulnerable all at once. "Well, we were thinking... You have such a great voice for storytelling, and you seem to know a lot of good tales. We thought maybe you could... I don't know, be the storyteller?"

The idea catches me off guard. Storytelling? In front of a crowd? It's not something I've done in years, not since Emily. She was the one who used to drag me to those kinds of things, getting me to read stories to kids or tell old folktales at the local fairs. It was never something I sought out, but with her, it was different. Everything was different.

"I don't know," I say, feeling that familiar anxiety creeping in. "I'm not really..."

"Logan, please," Lily interrupts, her eyes pleading. "You'd be perfect for it. And honestly, it would mean a lot to me if you did. This Bash... It's so important, and I just want everything to go well. I know it's asking a lot, but..."

She trails off, and I can see the uncertainty in her eyes, the fear that she's pushing too hard, asking too much of me. A flicker of doubt crosses her face, and I can almost feel the weight of her expectations pressing down on us. And just like that, my resolve weakens, slipping away like sand through my fingers. I don't want to disappoint her. I don't want to be the reason she feels like she failed. I've spent so long hiding from the world, but now, looking at Lily, I find myself wanting to step out of the shadows. Maybe it's because I see something in her that reminds me of Emily, or maybe it's something entirely different. Whatever it is, I can't seem to say no.

"Alright," I say, the word coming out before I can second-guess it. "I'll do it."

Lily's face lights up, and the sight of her smile sends a jolt of warmth through me. "Really? Oh, thank you, Logan! You have no idea how much this means to me."

Her enthusiasm is contagious, and for the first time in a long while, I feel a flicker of something I thought I'd lost—hope. Hope that maybe, just maybe, there's still something out there for me. Something worth stepping back into the world for.

We spend the next hour diving into the details of the Bash, exchanging ideas and reminiscing about the stories I could share. Lily's excitement is palpable as she describes how the event is coming together, each detail adding to the tapestry of what promises to be an unforgettable evening. I can see the passion in her eyes, and it ignites a spark in me, urging me to contribute my own experiences and insights to the conversation.

The conversation flows effortlessly, comfortable and warm, punctuated by moments of genuine laughter that resonate with familiarity. Yet, beneath this light-hearted exchange, there's an undercurrent of tension—a burgeoning awareness of the connection that is quietly blossoming between us. It remains unspoken, but it lingers, palpable in the silences that stretch between our words, in the way our eyes meet and hold just a fraction too long, as if daring the other to acknowledge the depth of what's unfolding.

As she gets ready to leave, I walk her to the door, my heart still racing from the time we've spent together. "I'll have the pumpkins ready in a few days," I tell her, my voice steady despite the turmoil inside.

"Thanks, Logan," she says, her smile soft and genuine. "And thank you for agreeing to the storytelling. I appreciate it."

I nod, not trusting myself to say anything more. As she steps outside, the cool air rushes in, enveloping me in a brisk embrace that feels like a jolt to my senses, a stark contrast to the warmth of her presence that lingers in the space we shared. I watch her walk away, that same pull I felt the first time we met growing stronger, more insistent, like an invisible thread tethering me to her. It terrifies me, this feeling, a mix of exhilaration and dread swirling in my chest. But at the same time, I can't seem to pull away, as if the very act of letting go would mean losing a part of myself I didn't know I had found.

I close the door and my mind starts racing. This wasn't supposed to happen. I wasn't supposed to care again, to feel this way again. But here I am, caring too much, feeling too much. And for the first time in years, I'm not sure if that's such a bad thing.

CHAPTER 5

Lily

THE LATE AFTERNOON sun filters through the windows of the Buttercup Inn, casting a warm, golden glow over the wooden floors. I take a deep breath, trying to steady my nerves as I roll out dough for another batch of pies. The kitchen, usually my sanctuary, feels different today. There's a tension in the air that I can't quite shake, a sense of unease that's been lingering ever since my encounter with Mrs. Whittaker earlier this morning.

She'd stopped by the Inn, as she often does, under the pretense of checking in on how the Bash preparations were going. But as always, there was something else behind her sharp eyes and even sharper tongue. Mrs. Whittaker was one of my grandmother's closest friends, and she never hesitates to remind me of that. Today was no different.

"Margaret would have had the whole town buzzing by now," she'd said, her voice dripping with that familiar mix of pity and condescension she'd perfected over the years. It was as if she took a twisted pleasure in reminding me of my grandmother's legacy, as though every word was a pointed reminder of my supposed inadequacies in living up to Margaret Thompson's grand reputation. "She always knew how to bring people together. It's a shame she's not here to see this year's Bash. I'm sure she would have made it something special."

The words cut deeper than I'd like to admit. I know she didn't mean them as a direct insult, but the implication was clear: I'm not my grandmother, and I never will be. As much as I've tried to fill her shoes, to live up to the legacy she left behind, there's always that nagging doubt in the back of my mind —what if I'm not good enough? What if I let everyone down?

I press my palms into the dough, trying to work out my frustration. The kitchen smells of cinnamon and apples, a scent that usually brings me comfort, reminding me of the countless hours I spent here with my grandmother, learning her recipes, listening to her stories. But today, the scent only serves to heighten the pressure I feel. I have to make this Bash a success. I have to prove to myself—and to everyone else—that I can do this.

But even as I try to focus on the task at hand, my thoughts drift back to Logan. There's something about him that I can't quite put my finger on. Ever since that first meeting at his cabin, I've been increasingly drawn to him. His quiet strength, his ruggedness, the way he looks at me with those intense blue eyes—it all makes my heart race in a way I haven't felt in a long time. But there's also a part of me that's afraid. Afraid that I'm reading too much into our interactions, that he doesn't feel the same way, that I'm setting myself up for disappointment.

I sigh, glancing at the clock. Greg should be here any minute. He's been my lifeline these past few weeks, always here with a supportive word or a joke to lighten the mood. I don't know what I'd do without him, especially on days like this when the doubts start creeping in.

As if on cue, I hear the front door creak open, followed by the warm and familiar sound of Greg's voice echoing from the foyer, his tone bright and inviting as he calls out my name. "Lily, where are you? I've got something you need to try!"

"In the kitchen!" I call back, trying to inject some cheer into my voice. I can hear the smile in his voice as he steps into the room, holding up a plate of cookies.

"Fresh out of the oven," he says, setting the plate on the counter. "I think these might be my best batch yet."

I smile, grateful for the distraction. "They smell amazing."

He grins, reaching for one of the cookies and taking a bite. "You know, I've been thinking about the Pumpkin Pie Contest. We should add a special category in honor of your grandmother. Something that highlights what she was all about."

I pause, considering it. "That's a great idea, Greg. She always took so much pride in that contest. It would be nice to do something special for her."

"Exactly," he says, leaning against the counter. "We could call it the Margaret Thompson Memorial Award or something like that. People could enter pies that use her recipes or maybe even their own takes on them. It would be a great way to keep her memory alive."

I nod slowly, feeling a wave of emotion rise within me, a bittersweet mix of nostalgia and gratitude. Greg always seems to know exactly what to say to strike a chord in my heart, and in moments like these, his words wrap around me like a warm embrace, reminding me of all that my grandmother meant to both of us. "I think she would have loved that."

Greg's smile softens as he watches me, and I can see the concern in his eyes. "Hey, don't let Mrs. Whittaker get to you. You're doing an amazing job, Lily. I know it's a lot of pressure, but your grandmother believed in you, and so do I."

I swallow hard, trying to keep the tears at bay. "Thanks, Greg. It's just... It's hard sometimes, you know? I want to make her proud, but I keep worrying that I'm going to mess it all up."

"You're not going to mess it up," he says firmly. "You've got this. And you're not alone. I'm here, and so is the rest of the town. We're all behind you."

His words are a balm to my frazzled nerves, and I take a deep breath, feeling some of the tension start to ease. "Thanks, Greg. I really needed to hear that."

He gives me a reassuring nod. "Anytime. And speaking of support, how are things going with Logan? Have you asked him to be a judge yet?"

I feel my cheeks warm at the mention of Logan's name. "Not yet. I was going to ask him later today."

Greg's grin widens. "Good. You two seem to be getting along well."

"Yeah, we are," I admit, though my heart starts to race just thinking about it. "I'm just... I don't know. I'm nervous."

"Nervous about what?" Greg asks, his tone light but curious.

"Nervous that he'll say no. Nervous that I'm pushing him too much," I say, the words spilling out before I can stop them. "And maybe nervous because... because I'm starting to care about what he thinks. About him."

Greg's expression softens even more, a gentle warmth spreading across his face. He leans in slightly, reaching out to squeeze my shoulder in a reassuring gesture, as if to let me know that I'm not alone in this moment of vulnerability. "Lily, it's okay to care. You deserve to be happy, and if Logan makes you happy, that's a good thing. Don't be afraid to follow your heart."

I take a deep breath, letting his words sink in. Maybe he's right. Maybe it's okay to let myself care and see where this thing with Logan might lead. "Thanks, Greg."

"Anytime," he says with a wink. "Now, go ask him. I've got a good feeling about this."

I nod, feeling a mix of nerves and excitement as I wipe my hands on a towel and head for the door.

The drive to Logan's cabin feels longer today, every mile heavy with anticipation. My heart races as I approach the door, and I have to remind myself to breathe.

When I knock, Logan answers almost immediately, as if he's been waiting for me. He looks surprised but pleased to see me, his blue eyes softening as he takes me in. "Lily. What brings you by?"

I swallow, trying to find my voice. "I wanted to talk to you about the Pumpkin Pie Contest. We're adding a special category in honor of my grandmother, and I was wondering if... if you'd like to be one of the judges."

There's a moment of silence as he considers my request, and I can't help but feel a flutter of anxiety. What if he says no? What if he doesn't want to be involved?

But then he nods, a small smile playing at the corners of his mouth. "I'd be honored."

Relief floods through me, and I can't help the smile that spreads across my face. "Thank you, Logan. That means a lot to me."

"Anytime," he says, echoing Greg's words from earlier, and I feel a warmth in my chest that's both comforting and terrifying at the same time. There's something here, between us, something that feels important, and I'm starting to realize that I want to explore it, to see where it might lead.

But for now, I focus on the task at hand, on making the Bash a success. And with Logan by my side, maybe, just maybe, I can do it.

CHAPTER 6

Logan

THE PARLOR of the Buttercup Inn is warm and inviting, a stark contrast to the cold, dark nights that are growing longer with each passing day. The fire crackles in the hearth, its flames dancing and casting long, flickering shadows across the walls. The plush armchairs, the soft rugs underfoot, the gentle glow of the firelight—all of it combines to create an atmosphere that's both cozy and intimate. It's the kind of setting that encourages you to let your guard down, to share things you might otherwise keep hidden.

And that's exactly what I've been doing.

I glance at Lily, who's settled into the armchair across from me, her legs tucked beneath her as she listens intently. Her eyes are bright, reflecting the firelight, and she's got that look again—the one that makes it impossible not to keep talking, to keep sharing. It's been like this for the past few nights. We've been meeting here to practice the stories for the Halloween Bash, but somewhere along the way, these sessions have become about more than just the stories.

They've become about us.

At first, I was hesitant. I'm not used to opening up, to letting anyone in, especially not someone like Lily. She's different. She's... warm. She makes me feel things I haven't felt in years—things I'm not sure I'm ready to feel again. But being around her, talking with her, it makes me feel alive in a way I didn't think was possible anymore. It's terrifying, but it's also something I can't seem to resist.

I lean back in my chair, the flickering firelight casting shadows on the walls, and begin another story. This one is a ghost tale my mother used to tell me when I was a kid. It's the kind of story that would send shivers down your spine, but there's also a warmth to it, a familiarity that comes from the memories attached to it. As I speak, I find myself slipping into the past, remembering the way my mother's voice would lower to a whisper during the spookier parts, how she'd laugh when I'd jump at the twists in the tale.

Lily's eyes widen with an almost childlike wonder as I reach the climax of the story, her hands clutching the edge of the soft, cozy blanket draped over her lap with a sense of urgency. I can't help but smile at her reaction, feeling a strange mix of nostalgia and warmth wash over me, as if I could almost hear my mother's voice echoing in the background, encouraging me to keep the tale alive. It's been so long since I've shared stories with anyone. I never thought I'd have the chance again.

When I finish, the room falls into a comfortable silence, broken only by the crackling of the fire. Lily looks at me, her expression thoughtful.

"Your mother told you that one?" she asks softly.

I nod, the memories still vivid in my mind. "Yeah. She had a whole collection of ghost stories she used to tell me and my brothers when we were kids. This one was my favorite."

There's a moment of silence as Lily processes this,

her gaze never leaving mine. "It's a beautiful story. A little eerie, but beautiful."

"It is," I agree, my voice quiet. "It's strange, though. Telling these stories again, it feels like I'm... reconnecting with something I thought I'd lost."

Lily's expression softens, and she leans forward slightly, her eyes searching mine. "I think it's wonderful that you're sharing them with me, with everyone. It's like you're keeping those memories alive."

I look down at my hands, feeling a rush of emotions that I'm not quite sure how to handle. She's right, of course. Sharing these stories, opening up to Lily —it's like I'm bringing a part of myself back to life, a part I thought was gone forever. But with that comes the fear, the ever-present worry that if I let myself care too much, I'll lose it all again. I'm not sure I can survive that a second time.

"Sometimes," I start, hesitating before continuing, "sometimes it's easier to keep things buried, to not think about them too much."

"But does that really make them go away?" Lily asks gently. "Or does it just make the pain linger longer?"

I glance up at her, taken aback by the insight in her words. She's right again, but it's not something I'm ready to admit. Instead, I give her a small smile, trying to deflect. "You're too wise for your own good, you know that?"

She laughs softly, the sound like a balm to my frayed nerves. "I'm just trying to help."

"And you are," I say, meeting her gaze. "More than you know."

There's a moment where neither of us speaks, a silence that stretches between us like a taut string. I can feel the tension building, a palpable energy humming in the air, the growing awareness of what's happening between us. It's been there from the start, an unspoken bond, this pull, this connection that seems to grow stronger with every passing day, weaving itself into the very fabric of our interactions. Each shared glance and soft laugh only deepens the awareness, making it harder to ignore the emotions swirling just beneath the surface. But with it comes the fear—the fear of what might happen if I let myself feel this, if I let myself care again.

I'm falling for her. I know it, even if I'm not ready to say it out loud. Every time I see her, every time we talk, that pull becomes harder to resist. It's like she's breaking down the walls I've spent years building, brick by brick, with nothing more than a smile and a kind word.

But the closer I get to her, the more I realize how much I have to lose. And that terrifies me.

"I should probably get going," I say finally, breaking the silence. "It's getting late."

Lily's face falls slightly, the light in her green eyes dimming for a moment, but she nods, her expression shifting to one of understanding. It's as if she recognizes the weight of my words, the unspoken fears that linger between us. "Of course. We can pick this up again tomorrow."

I stand up, feeling a pang of regret as I do. I don't want to leave, but I know I need to. I need some space, some time to think, to sort through everything I'm feeling. But even as I head for the door, I can feel the pull of her presence, the way it tugs at me, making me want to stay.

"Logan?" she calls softly, just as I'm about to step out.

I turn back to her, my heart pounding in my chest. "Yeah?"

"Thank you," she says, her voice full of sincerity. "For everything. I really appreciate it."

I give her a small smile, trying to keep my emotions in check. "Anytime, Lily."

As I step outside into the cool night air, I take a deep breath, the crispness filling my lungs and helping to clear my mind. I close my eyes for a moment, trying to steady myself, to shake off the weight of the emotions that have been swirling inside me. The gentle rustle of leaves and the distant chirp of crickets provide a soothing backdrop, reminding me that the world keeps moving, even as I stand still, grappling with my thoughts. My heart is still racing, and I can feel the familiar swirl of emotions—fear, excitement, longing— -all competing for attention. I know I'm falling for her, and I know it's dangerous. But at the same time, I can't seem to help it.

I head back to my cabin, the cool night air blowing through my truck's window, doing little to calm the storm inside me. I can still see her face in my mind, still hear her voice, and with every mile I drive, I feel that pull getting stronger.

I'm falling for her. And as terrifying as that is, I can't help but want more.

CHAPTER 7

Lily

THE SKY IS a deep shade of twilight, the first stars just beginning to twinkle as I stand in the town square, surrounded by the warm glow of lanterns. The air is filled with the sound of laughter and conversation, the hum of the community coming together in a way that feels almost magical. The Lantern-Making Workshop is in full swing, and for the first time in days, I feel a sense of calm washing over me.

But it's fragile, this calm. Beneath it, the doubts are still there, lurking just below the surface, ready to pull me under if I let them. The pressure of the Bash, the weight of living up to my grandmother's legacy—it all feels like too much at times. Mrs.

Whittaker's words from the other day still sting, echoing in my mind when I least expect it.

"Margaret would have done it this way," she'd said, her tone sharp as she eyed the decorations I'd chosen for the town square. "She had a way of bringing people together, you know. A real gift."

I'd smiled and nodded, trying to brush it off, but the words cut deep. What if she's right? What if the townspeople will always see me as a lesser version of my grandmother? What if I'm not good enough to fill her shoes?

I let out a slow breath, feeling the weight of the negativity begin to lift, even if just a little. This is supposed to be a joyful occasion, a chance for the community to come together, to share laughter, and to create something beautiful that everyone can cherish. I need to focus on that. I need to believe that I'm doing my best, that my best is enough to honor the legacy of those who came before me and to make my own mark in this town.

"Lily, these lanterns are turning out great!" Greg's voice cuts through the haze of my thoughts, jolting me back to the present moment. I turn to see him striding towards me, a wide grin stretching across his face, radiating infectious enthusiasm. In his hands, he carries a finished lantern, its intricate design shimmering softly as it catches the last rays of the fading light. The delicate patterns etched into its surface seem to dance, reflecting the warmth of the gathering dusk.

"Thanks, Greg," I say, managing a smile. "They really are beautiful."

He gives me a knowing look as if he can see right through the mask I'm trying to wear. "You're doing an amazing job, you know that? Your grandmother would be proud."

His words hit me square in the chest, and I feel a lump forming in my throat. I swallow hard, trying to keep my emotions in check. "I hope so."

"She would be," Greg insists, his tone gentle but firm. "And you need to stop doubting yourself. You've put so much heart into this Halloween Bash, and everyone can see it. You're making it your own, Lily, and that's what matters."

I nod, though the doubts still cling to the edges of my mind. "Thanks, Greg. I really needed to hear that."

"Anytime," he says with a wink. "Now, go check out Logan's station. He's got the whole town mesmerized with his lanterns."

At the mention of Logan's name, my heart skips a beat. I turn to look across the square, where Logan is standing with a group of townspeople, guiding them through the process of carving intricate designs into the lanterns. The firelight dances across his face, highlighting the strong lines of his jaw, the intensity in his blue eyes as he concentrates on his work. There's a quiet confidence about him, a steadiness that seems to draw people in, and I can see the townspeople responding to it, hanging on his every word.

As I watch him, I feel a warmth spread through my chest, mingling with the remnants of my anxiety. Logan's been a constant source of support these past few days, always there with a reassuring word or a steady presence when I needed it most. He's shared stories of his own struggles with self-doubt, stories that have made me feel less alone in my fears. And more than that, he's made me feel like I can do this, like I'm not just filling my grandmother's shoes but creating something of my own.

I make my way over to his station, weaving through the crowd until I'm standing beside him. He looks up as I approach, a small smile tugging at the corners of his mouth. "Hey, Lily. How's it going?"

"Good," I say, though the word feels inadequate. "Really good. The workshop is a success."

"That's all thanks to you," he says, his voice low and steady.

I shake my head, feeling a warm blush creep up my cheeks, spreading like the first light of dawn. It's a mix of embarrassment and something else—perhaps excitement—that sends a flutter through my stomach. "It's not just me. It's everyone coming together, helping out. Including you."

He holds my gaze for a moment, his eyes searching mine. There's something in his expression, something that makes my heart race and my breath catch in my throat. "You've done something special here, Lily. Your grandmother would be proud."

The sincerity in his voice, combined with the quiet intensity of his gaze, feels almost overwhelming. It stirs something deep within me, a mix of vulnerability and exhilaration that threatens to spill over. I quickly look away, my heart racing, and direct my attention to the lantern he's meticulously working on. The flickering candlelight casts playful shadows around us, providing a welcome distraction as I attempt to steady myself and regain my composure. "Thank you, Logan. That means a lot."

There's a brief silence, one that feels charged with all the things we're not saying. I can feel the tension between us, the growing connection that's been building with each passing day. It's both exhilarating and terrifying, this pull I feel toward him, this sense that something significant is happening between us.

"Want to try?" Logan's voice pulls me back to the present, and I realize he's holding out the carving tool to me, offering me a chance to work on the lantern.

I hesitate for a moment before taking the carving tool from him, my fingers brushing against his as I do. That brief touch sends a spark, a jolt of electricity surging through me, igniting a warmth that radiates from the point of contact. I can sense that he feels it, too, the way his breath catches slightly as our hands meet. Yet, despite the palpable energy crackling between us, neither of us says anything, both of us choosing to remain focused on the task at hand, each lost in our thoughts and the unspoken tension that lingers in the air around us.

As I carve into the lantern, Logan guides me, his voice low and soothing, his presence a steadying force beside me. The world around us seems to fade away, leaving just the two of us in the warm glow of the lanterns, the sound of our quiet breaths mingling with the crackle of the firelight.

For the first time in a long while, I feel a sense of peace, a feeling that maybe, just maybe, I'm on the right path. The doubts are still there, but they're quieter now, overshadowed by the warmth of Logan's support, by the sense of community that's grown around this event.

When we finish the lantern, I step back, admiring the intricate design we've created together. It's beautiful, glowing softly in the twilight, a symbol of everything this Bash has come to represent—community, connection, and the possibility of something new.

"Thank you, Logan," I say softly, turning to look at him. "For everything."

He meets my gaze, his expression serious but warm. "Anytime, Lily."

There's a moment where I think he might say more, where I think we might finally acknowledge the growing bond between us. But before either of us can speak, we're interrupted by a group of children rushing over, eager to show off their finished lanterns.

The moment passes, but the warmth remains, a quiet, comforting presence that lingers long after Logan and I part ways for the evening.

As I walk back to the Inn, the glow of the lanterns lighting my way, I feel a sense of hope blossoming in my chest. The Bash is coming together, the community is rallying around me, and for the first time, I'm starting to believe that I can do this—that I'm not just living in my grandmother's shadow, but creating a legacy of my own.

And maybe, just maybe, there's room in that legacy for something more—something that feels a lot like the beginning of love.

CHAPTER 8

Logan

THE TOWN SQUARE is alive in a way I've never seen before. The colors and scents of autumn fill the air—the rich golds, reds, and oranges of the leaves scattered across the ground, the sharp, clean smell of pine, and the warm, earthy aroma of freshly cut wood. The usually quiet square is bustling with activity, the warmth of the community spirit palpable as townspeople gather around tables laden with supplies, eager to learn the art of lantern-making.

I take a deep breath, letting the familiar scents ground me as I focus on the task at hand. It's been a long time since I've felt this kind of energy, this sense of connection to the people around me. And it's all because of Lily.

She's done something incredible here, bringing the town together in a way that feels effortless, and natural. As I guide a group of children through the process of carving intricate designs into their lanterns, I can't help but steal glances at her across the square. She's moving from table to table, offering words of encouragement, her smile bright and genuine. The lanterns glow softly in the fading light, reflecting the warmth that she's brought to this event, to this town.

And to me.

The thought sends a jolt through me, a mix of exhilaration and fear. I've been trying to keep my feelings for Lily at bay, trying to convince myself that I'm just falling for the idea of her, that this is just infatuation. But the truth is, I'm not just falling for her—I'm already deeply in love with her. And it terrifies me.

I focus on the lantern in front of me, my hands moving automatically as I carve the design, but my mind is elsewhere. I've never been one to take risks, especially when it comes to matters of the heart. Losing Emily was a blow I barely survived, and the thought of opening myself up to that kind of pain again—it's almost too much to bear.

But then I look up and see Lily laughing with one of the townspeople, her auburn hair catching the soft glow of the lantern light and her green eyes sparkling with a contagious joy that warms my heart. In that moment, I realize that no matter how hard I try to maintain my distance, to shield myself from potential heartache, I can't walk away from this connection. I can't walk away from her. The pull is too strong, an invisible thread that tugs at my very being, drawing me closer to the light and laughter that she effortlessly radiates.

As the evening progresses, the square becomes a hive of activity, filled with the sounds of laughter, conversation, and the steady rhythm of carving tools against wood. The lanterns are starting to take shape, each one a unique work of art, and the pride in the faces of the townspeople is unmistakable.

I notice Mrs. Whittaker standing at the edge of the square, her arms crossed and her posture rigid as she observes the proceedings with a critical eye. She's been skeptical of Lily's plans from the beginning, her doubts lingering like a shadow over the festivities, and I can see the lines of concern still etched on her face. But as the evening wears on and the atmosphere grows more vibrant, something shifts within her. Her gaze softens, almost imperceptibly, as she watches Lily weave effortlessly through the crowd, her auburn hair catching the warm glow of the lanterns. Then, in a surprising turn, her attention shifts to me, a flicker of contemplation passing through her eyes.

I keep working, but I can feel her eyes on me, evaluating and judging. It makes me uneasy at first —Mrs. Whittaker is not someone you easily impress. But as I finish up another lantern and hand it to a little girl who beams up at me with pride, I catch a glimpse of something unexpected in Mrs. Whittaker's expression—approval.

By the end of the night, she's approached me, her critical demeanor noticeably softer. "You've done a fine job here tonight, Logan," she says, her voice lacking its usual sharpness. "And so has Lily. I wasn't sure at first, but... well, she's proven herself."

The words take me by surprise, and I glance over at Lily, who's standing nearby, oblivious to our conversation. "She has," I agree, feeling a swell of pride in my chest. "She's stronger than she thinks."

Mrs. Whittaker nods, her gaze following mine. "That she is. Margaret would be proud."

The simple statement holds a weight that I know Lily has been carrying since she took on this responsibility. Hearing Mrs. Whittaker—Margaret's old friend, the town's harshest critic—acknowledge Lily's success is no small thing. It reassures me that Lily is more than capable of handling this, of handling anything. But it also deepens the fear that's been gnawing at me since the start—what if I let her in, and then lose her, just like I lost Emily?

I don't have an answer for that, and it's a fear I can't easily shake. But for now, I push it aside, focusing instead on the task at hand, on the connection that's growing between Lily and me, and the warmth that fills the square.

As the workshop winds down, I find myself working side by side with Lily. We don't say much at first; both of us focused on the lanterns, but the silence between us is comfortable and filled with the unspoken understanding that's been building between us.

Occasionally, our hands brush against each other as we pass tools back and forth, and each time, there's an unmistakable spark—a quiet, electric charge that I sense she feels, too. It's evident in the way her eyes meet mine, holding my gaze for just a heartbeat longer than necessary, in the way her smile lingers a fraction longer as if she's savoring the moment. The air around us feels charged with possibility, and the space between us seems to shrink with each passing moment, drawing us closer together in this shared experience.

At one point, as we're both leaning over the same lantern, our hands busy with delicate tools, I find myself beginning to share a story from my childhood—a vivid memory of my father patiently guiding me as I carved my first piece of wood, the scent of fresh shavings filling the air. It's a tale I haven't recounted in years, tucked away in a corner of my mind, but with Lily, it flows effortlessly, as if the words were waiting for the right moment to escape. She listens intently, her eyes never leaving mine, shining with a genuine interest that warms my heart. The way her expression softens as I speak reassures me that this moment, this connection, is something special.

"That's a beautiful memory, Logan," she says softly when I finish. "Thank you for sharing it with me."

The sincerity in her voice, the way she looks at me —it's almost too much. I can feel my heart pounding in my chest, the weight of my emotions pressing down on me, but it's not an unpleasant feeling. It's just... overwhelming.

We finish the lantern together, and as we step back to admire it, I realize that the connection between us has deepened in ways I hadn't anticipated. It's not just about attraction anymore—though that's certainly there—it's about something more. Something that feels like love.

The thought both exhilarates and terrifies me. I'm falling in love with Lily, and as much as I want to let myself feel it and embrace it, there's a part of me that's holding back and afraid of what might happen if I do.

But then I look at her, standing beside me, the soft glow of the lanterns illuminating her face, and I know that I can't keep denying what's happening between us. I can't keep running from this, from her.

As the evening comes to a close, and the townspeople start to pack up their things, I catch Mrs. Whittaker speaking with Lily. I can't hear what she's saying, but I see the way Lily's face lights up, the way she nods, her expression filled with a mix of relief and gratitude. It's clear that Mrs. Whittaker's skepticism has finally melted away, replaced by a newfound respect for Lily's leadership and determination.

I feel a sense of pride and admiration for Lily that I can't quite put into words. She's done something incredible tonight, something I know Margaret would be proud of. But more than that, she's shown me that she's not just capable—she's remarkable.

As we finish cleaning up, I find myself lingering by Lily's side, not wanting the night to end. There's so much I want to say, so much I want to express, but the words don't come. Instead, I let the silence speak for me, let the quiet moments of connection and shared glances convey what I'm feeling.

"Thank you, Logan," Lily says softly as we stand in the now-empty square, the last of the lanterns glowing softly around us. "For everything."

"Anytime, Lily," I reply, my voice equally soft. There's so much more I want to say, but I hold back, not ready to open that door just yet.

As we part ways, I can't help but feel a sense of anticipation for what's to come. I know that this is just the beginning, that there's so much more ahead for us—if I'm brave enough to take that step, to let myself fall completely.

And maybe, just maybe, I'm ready to try.

CHAPTER 9

Lily

AFTER LAST NIGHT'S successful lantern event, I went to bed on cloud nine. But a storm hit Buttercup Bay hard last night, and the damage is worse than I feared. As I walk through the town square, my heart sinks at the sight of broken lanterns, toppled decorations, and soaked banners. The bright, cheerful colors that had once filled the square are now a sodden, tangled mess. The Halloween Bash is just days away, and everything feels like it's suddenly falling apart.

I take a deep breath, trying to steady myself, but the pressure is overwhelming. The town's expectations, the legacy of my grandmother, the fear of failing in front of everyone—especially Mrs. Whittaker and

Mayor Thompson—it all feels like too much. For the first time since I started this journey, I seriously consider giving up.

As these thoughts swirl in my mind, a wave of helplessness washes over me. I feel tears prickling at the corners of my eyes, but I force them back. I can't afford to break down, not now. But as I look around at the damage, I can't see a way out. I can't see how I'm going to pull this off.

"Lily?" Logan's voice slices through the storm of my thoughts, steady and calm, like a lighthouse guiding me back to shore. I turn to see him walking toward me, his expression serious yet carrying a warmth in his eyes that immediately soothes some of the panic swirling in my chest. The world around us seems to fade for a moment, leaving just the two of us in this chaotic moment, and I find myself drawn to the reassurance he offers, as if he knows exactly what I'm feeling.

"Logan..." My voice wavers as I try to explain, but I can't find the words. All I can do is gesture helplessly at the wreckage around us.

He takes it all in with a quick, assessing glance, then

turns back to me, his expression unwavering. "It's okay. We'll fix this."

"How?" I ask, the desperation clear in my voice. "There's so much to do, and the Bash is so close, and—"

"Hey," Logan interrupts gently, stepping closer and placing a reassuring hand on my shoulder. "You're not alone in this. We'll get through it together."

There's something in the way he says it, something in the quiet confidence of his tone that makes me believe him. For the first time since the storm hit, I feel a glimmer of hope. Logan's presence is like an anchor, grounding me, reminding me that I don't have to do this alone.

He turns toward the square, already starting to formulate a plan. "Let's get everyone together. We'll organize a cleanup, get the decorations repaired or replaced, and make sure everything's ready in time."

I nod, feeling a spark of determination reignite inside me. "Okay. Let's do it."

With Logan leading the charge, the townspeople quickly rally. It's amazing to see how his quiet leadership inspires everyone around him. He doesn't have to shout or give orders—just his presence and calm assurance are enough to get people moving, to make them believe that this is possible.

As the day progresses, the square slowly starts to come back to life, shedding its earlier gloom like a snake shedding its skin. Broken lanterns are replaced with new ones that gleam brightly in the daylight, their warm glow promising a sense of hope. Soaked banners are swapped out for fresh, dry fabric, their vibrant colors fluttering in the gentle breeze, reminiscent of the joy that once filled this space. The decorations are lovingly repaired and rehung, each one a testament to the resilience of our community spirit. There's still so much to do —tasks looming like shadows on the horizon—but with each small victory we achieve, I feel my confidence returning, growing stronger and more vibrant, just like the square itself.

Logan is everywhere, helping where he's needed, offering guidance and support. And each time our paths cross, he gives me a small, encouraging smile that helps keep my fears at bay. I'm acutely aware of how much I've come to rely on him, not just as a partner in planning the Bash, but as someone who has become incredibly important to me.

But with that realization comes another—deeper and more frightening. I'm falling for Logan. Hard. And the thought both excites and terrifies me. I've never felt this way about anyone before, and the intensity of it is almost overwhelming. I wonder if he feels the same way, but the fear of ruining what we have keeps me from asking.

As the sun begins to dip below the horizon, casting a soft golden glow across the landscape, I find myself back at the Buttercup Inn with Logan. The parlor is warm and inviting, the fire crackling softly in the hearth, its glow dancing across the walls and creating a snug atmosphere. The events of the day have left me utterly exhausted, both physically and emotionally, but alongside that fatigue is a profound sense of accomplishment—a wave of relief washes over me as I reflect on how we managed to pull everything together despite the challenges we faced. The familiar scent of woodsmoke mingles with the delicate aroma of freshly brewed tea, wrapping me in a comforting embrace as I steal a glance at Logan, feeling grateful for his unwavering support.

We sit by the fire, the silence between us filled with unspoken emotions. I can feel the tension, the awareness of the growing connection between us, and it's all I can do to keep myself from blurting out everything I'm feeling. But I'm too afraid—afraid that if I say something, it will change everything, and I can't risk losing what we have.

Logan leans back in his chair, his gaze fixed on the fire. There's a contemplative look on his face, one that makes me wonder if he's thinking the same thing I am. If he's feeling the same pull, the same fear of what might happen if we let this go further.

"I've been thinking," he says suddenly, breaking the silence. His voice is low, thoughtful. "About what you said earlier, about feeling like you're not good enough. I just want you to know... you're doing an amazing job, Lily. The Bash, the way you've brought everyone together—it's incredible. You should be proud of what you've accomplished."

His words are like a balm to my soul, easing the last remnants of doubt that have been plaguing me all day. "Thank you, Logan," I say softly, my heart full of gratitude and something deeper, something I'm almost afraid to name. "I couldn't have done any of this without you."

"You could have," he replies, his gaze meeting mine. "But I'm glad you didn't have to."

The air between us is thick with unspoken words, with the tension of everything we're not saying. I can feel my heart pounding in my chest, the weight of my emotions pressing down on me. This is the moment, the perfect time to say something, to tell him how I feel. But the fear is still there, holding me back, keeping me from taking that leap.

Instead, I just smile at him, a small, tentative smile that I hope conveys at least a fraction of what I'm feeling. "I'm glad you were here," I say quietly.

Logan's eyes soften, and for a moment, I think he might say something more, something that will break this tension between us once and for all. But he doesn't. Instead, he just nods, his gaze lingering on mine for a long, charged moment before he turns back to the fire.

The silence that follows is comfortable, but there's an undercurrent of longing, of things left unsaid. I know I need to say something, to take the risk and tell him how I feel, but the words won't come. The fear of what might happen if I do—if he doesn't feel the same way, if it ruins everything—keeps me silent.

Eventually, Logan stands, stretching slightly before looking down at me. "It's late. We should probably get some rest. Tomorrow's another big day."

I nod, standing as well, though part of me doesn't want the evening to end. "You're right. We need to be ready for the Bash."

He walks me to the door, and for a moment, we just stand there, the firelight casting long shadows across the room. There's so much I want to say, so much I want to express, but the fear is still there, holding me back.

"Goodnight, Lily," Logan says softly, his voice full of warmth and something else, something I can't quite name.

"Goodnight, Logan," I reply, my heart aching with everything I'm not saying.

As he leaves, I'm left standing in the doorway, watching him disappear into the night. The warmth of the fire is still there, but the room feels suddenly empty, as if something vital has just slipped through my fingers.

I know I need to tell him how I feel. I know I need to take the risk, to let him in. But for now, all I can do is stand here, my heart full of unspoken emotions, hoping that when the time comes, I'll find the courage to tell him the truth.

CHAPTER 10

Logan

THE CABIN IS QUIET, save for the steady rhythm of my knife carving into the pumpkin. The fire crackles softly in the hearth, casting a warm, flickering glow across the room. It's a familiar scene—one I've found comfort in for years—but tonight, there's an undercurrent of tension that I can't shake. My thoughts keep drifting back to Lily, to the way she smiled at me today, to the way she looked at me when she thought I wasn't watching.

I pause, the knife hovering over the pumpkin as a wave of emotion washes over me. It's like a dam has broken inside me, and everything I've been trying to keep at bay—my feelings for Lily, the fear of losing her, the memories of Emily—comes rushing to the surface all at once. I feel like I'm standing on the edge of a cliff, staring down into the unknown, torn between the desire to leap and the instinct to protect myself from the fall.

Emily's face flashes in my mind, a bittersweet memory that brings with it a familiar ache. Losing her was the hardest thing I've ever been through, and the thought of opening myself up to that kind of pain again—it's almost too much to bear. But then I think of Lily, of the way she's brought light and warmth back into my life, and I know that keeping myself closed off isn't the answer. It won't protect me from pain—it will only keep me from experiencing the love and joy that she's brought into my world.

I set the knife down, running a hand through my hair as I let out a slow breath. I've been a coward, hiding behind my grief, using it as an excuse to keep people at a distance. But Lily deserves better than that. She deserves someone who's willing to take a chance, to risk everything for the possibility of something beautiful. And I want to be that someone.

I pick up the knife again, but this time, there's a new sense of purpose in my movements. With each cut, each careful stroke, I feel the weight lifting from my shoulders, replaced by a growing sense of clarity. I've made my decision. After the Bash, I'm going to tell Lily how I feel. No matter the risk, no matter the fear, I'm not going to let this chance slip away.

The night passes in a blur of focused work and quiet introspection. By the time the early hours of the morning roll around, I've finished the last of the pumpkins, each one carved with the same care and attention to detail that I've always prided myself on. But this time, there's something more—something that feels like hope.

I clean up the cabin, putting away my tools and setting the pumpkins aside for the Bash. There's a sense of calm that comes with the completion of the task, but beneath it, there's an undercurrent of anticipation, of nervous energy that has nothing to do with the event itself and everything to do with what I plan to do afterward.

As the first light of dawn begins to filter through the trees, I make my way to the Buttercup Inn. The town is still quiet, the streets empty and peaceful, but there's a sense of anticipation in the air as if the whole town is holding its breath, waiting for the Halloween Bash to begin.

When I arrive at the Inn, I find Lily in the parlor, going over the final details for the event. She looks up as I enter, and the smile that lights up her face is enough to make my heart skip a beat. There's something in her eyes—something soft and warm, but also a little uncertain—that makes me want to pull her into my arms and tell her everything right then and there. But I hold back, knowing that there's still work to be done.

"Hey," she says softly, her voice barely above a whisper, as she sets down her papers with a delicate touch. Her gaze meets mine, and I can see the warmth of her smile growing even brighter. "You're up early."

"Last-minute prep," I reply with a smile. "Wanted to make sure everything was ready."

She nods, her eyes scanning my face as if searching for something. "You look... different."

I raise an eyebrow, curious. "Different how?"

"I don't know," she says, her voice thoughtful. "You just seem... more at ease. Like something's shifted."

She's perceptive, as always. I can't help but smile at her observation, knowing she's right. Something has shifted—inside me, in the way I see things, in the way I feel. But I'm not ready to tell her just yet, not here, not now. "Maybe it has," I say softly, letting the words hang in the air between us.

There's a brief silence, one that feels charged with unspoken words, with the tension of everything we're not saying. I can see the questions in her eyes, the uncertainty, the hope, but before either of us can speak, she shakes her head as if brushing the thoughts away.

"We need to finalize a few details for the Bash," she says, her tone shifting back to business. "There's still a lot to do."

"Let's do it," I agree, though my mind is only half on the tasks at hand. The other half is consumed with thoughts of what's to come, of the moment when I'll finally tell her how I feel.

We spend the next hour going over the plans, checking and rechecking every detail to make sure everything is perfect. There's a quiet efficiency to our work, a sense of mutual understanding that makes the process almost effortless. It's like we're in sync, moving through the motions with an ease that comes from working together, from knowing each other so well.

But beneath the surface, there's an undercurrent of something more—something that neither of us is ready to acknowledge just yet. I can feel it in the way our hands brush when we pass papers back and forth, in the way her eyes linger on mine a moment longer than necessary, in the way my heart races every time she smiles at me.

As we wrap up the last of the preparations, I can sense her nerves beginning to fray. The weight of the town's expectations, the pressure of living up to her grandmother's legacy—it's all pressing down on her, and I can see it in the way she bites her lip, in the way her hands fidget with the edge of the table.

"Hey," I say softly, reaching out to place a hand on hers, stilling her movements. "It's going to be okay. You've done an incredible job, Lily. The Bash is going to be amazing, and everyone's going to see how much heart you've put into this."

She looks up at me, her eyes wide and vulnerable, and my heart aches with the urge to pull her into my arms, to hold her close, and never let go. "Thank you, Logan," she whispers, her voice thick with emotion. "I don't know what I'd do without you."

"You don't have to," I reply, my voice just as soft. "I'm not going anywhere."

There's a moment where I think she might say something more, where the air between us feels thick with unspoken words, but then she just nods, a small, grateful smile playing at the corners of her mouth. "We should get some rest," she says, her tone reluctant but practical. "We've got a big day ahead of us."

"Yeah," I agree, though part of me doesn't want to leave her side. "We do."

We stand there for a moment longer, neither of us quite ready to move, but eventually, she steps back, breaking the connection between us. "Goodbye, Logan," she says softly, her eyes lingering on mine for just a second too long.

"Goodbye, Lily," I reply, my voice just as soft.

As I watch her walk away, a sense of anticipation fills me, mingling with the fear and the hope that's been building inside me all night. I know that tonight, everything will change. And for the first time, I'm ready for it.

THE HALLOWEEN BASH has officially begun, and Buttercup Bay feels like a different world—one filled with magic, warmth, and a sense of community that I've never felt so deeply before. Lanterns line the streets, casting a soft, golden glow over the town square, where the air is thick with the scent of spiced cider, baked goods, and the crispness of autumn leaves. The decorations, the laughter, the bustling energy—it's all come together in a way that feels almost surreal, like a dream I'm afraid to wake from.

As I walk through the square, taking it all in, I can't help but feel a swell of pride in my chest. This... this is what I've been working toward. This is the culmination of weeks of planning, of late nights and early mornings, of doubts and fears that, somehow, I've managed to push through. For the first time, I feel like I've truly accomplished something, something that matters.

People stop to greet me as I pass, their faces lit with smiles and excitement. Children dart between the stalls, their costumes fluttering in the breeze, while the older folks chat happily, mugs of cider warming their hands. The town is alive, vibrant in a way that makes my heart ache with joy. I did this. I brought this together. And the realization fills me with a sense of pride that's almost overwhelming.

The Pumpkin Pie Contest is about to start, and the square is buzzing with anticipation. The long table set up for the judges is already laden with pies— each one a work of art, crafted with care and love by the townspeople. Logan, Mrs. Whittaker, and Mayor Thompson stand off to the side, discussing the criteria for judging. I can see the seriousness in their expressions, the way they're taking this task to heart, and it makes me smile. This contest was always one of my grandmother's favorites, and seeing it carried on in her memory feels right.

As I step up to the microphone to deliver my speech, a wave of nerves hits me. My heart pounds in my chest, my palms are damp, and for a brief moment, I wonder if I can really do this. But then I look out at the crowd, at the faces of the people who have supported me, who have believed in me, and I find the courage to speak.

"Thank you all for being here tonight," I begin, my voice trembling slightly before it steadies. "This Halloween Bash means so much to me, and I know it meant the world to my grandmother, Margaret Thompson. She loved this town, and she loved bringing people together. I'm honored to continue that tradition, and I couldn't have done it without the support of every single one of you."

I pause, letting the words sink in, feeling the emotion welling up in my chest. "This event isn't just about Halloween—it's about community, about the connections we share and the memories we create together. My grandmother taught me that, and I hope that tonight, we can all feel a little bit of the magic she brought to this town."

As I speak, my eyes find Logan's in the crowd. He's watching me with an intensity that sends a warmth spreading through me. The look of pride on his face fills me with a sense of hope and reassurance, like a promise that everything will be okay. I hold his gaze for a moment longer, letting that connection steady me before I continue.

"I want to thank you all for your hard work, your dedication, and your belief in this event," I say, my voice strong with conviction. "Tonight is about celebrating what we've accomplished together, and I'm so grateful to be a part of this amazing community."

The crowd applauds, and I step back from the microphone, my heart pounding with a mix of relief and pride. I did it. I really did it.

The Pumpkin Pie Contest begins in earnest, with Logan, Mrs. Whittaker, and Mayor Thompson taking their seats at the judges' table. The air is thick with tension and excitement as each pie is presented, the judges carefully tasting and deliberating over each one. I watch from the sidelines, my heart still racing, but this time with excitement rather than nerves. This is what my grandmother loved—seeing the community come together, celebrating the simple joys of life.

After what feels like an eternity, the judges finally reach a decision. Mayor Thompson steps forward to announce the winner, his voice booming over the crowd as he praises the quality of the entries and the spirit of the competition. The winner is a local baker who beams with pride as she accepts her ribbon, and the crowd erupts into cheers and applause.

As the crowd disperses, Mrs. Whittaker approaches me. For a moment, I tense, unsure of what to expect. But then she smiles—a real, genuine smile—and I feel my breath catch in my throat.

"Lily, you did a fine job tonight," she says, her voice warm and sincere. "I'll admit, I had my doubts at first, but you've proven me wrong. Your grandmother would be proud."

The words hit me like a wave, and I feel a rush of emotion that I can barely contain. Mrs. Whittaker's approval, her acknowledgment—it's something I've been hoping for, even if I didn't fully realize it until now. I finally feel like I've earned my place here, like I'm not just living in my grandmother's shadow but creating something of my own.

"Thank you," I manage to say, my voice thick with emotion. "That means so much to me."

She nods, her sharp eyes softening as she takes my

hand and gives it a gentle squeeze. "You're doing just fine, Lily. Keep it up."

As she walks away, I feel a weight lift from my shoulders—a weight I hadn't even realized I was carrying. The approval of someone as respected (and feared) as Mrs. Whittaker is more than just a compliment—it's a validation of everything I've worked for, everything I've doubted about myself. It's the final piece I needed to believe that I really am capable of carrying on my grandmother's legacy.

I look around the square, at the lanterns glowing softly in the night, at the people laughing and celebrating, at the way the town has come alive with the spirit of the season, and I feel a deep, abiding sense of contentment. This is my home. This is where I belong.

As the evening winds down, I find myself gravitating toward Logan. He's standing by one of the lanterns, his expression thoughtful as he watches the last of the crowd disperse. When he sees me approaching, he smiles—a smile that makes my heart flutter in a way I'm starting to realize is becoming all too familiar.

"Hey," he says softly as I reach him. "You did an amazing job tonight, Lily."

"Thank you," I reply, my voice equally soft. "I couldn't have done it without you."

He shakes his head, his eyes full of warmth. "You did this, Lily. You brought everyone together. You made this happen."

There's a moment of silence, one that feels charged with unspoken words, with the weight of everything that's passed between us. I can feel the warmth of his gaze, the steadiness of his presence, and for the first time, I feel truly at peace.

"Logan," I begin, my voice barely above a whisper. "I—"

But before I can finish, the sound of laughter and celebration pulls our attention back to the square, and the moment slips away. Logan's smile deepens, as if he knows what I am going to say, but he doesn't press. Instead, he simply nods, a silent promise that there will be time—time for everything we need to say.

CHAPTER 12

Logan

THE FIRE CRACKLES SOFTLY, casting flickering shadows that dance across the faces of the crowd gathered around the Spooky Storytelling Corner. The air is cool, filled with the scent of pine and the faint rustle of leaves as the night settles over Buttercup Bay. It's the perfect setting for a night of eerie tales, and as I take my place at the center, I can feel the anticipation in the air—the collective breath of the audience waiting for the stories to begin.

For a moment, I let the silence linger, letting the tension build. It's been years since I've done this, since I've felt this kind of connection with an audience. The last time I told stories like this was with Emily, before everything changed. But tonight, it feels different. Tonight, it feels like I'm stepping back into a life I thought I'd lost forever, and for the first time in a long time, I'm not afraid of it.

I begin with a tale my mother used to tell—a story about a haunted forest, where the trees whisper secrets and the shadows come alive after dark. My voice is steady as I weave the tale, but inside, my emotions are a whirlwind. As I speak, I watch the faces in the crowd, the way their eyes widen with each twist in the story, the way they lean in closer as the tension builds. It's a feeling I've missed, this connection, this shared experience of storytelling that binds us together, if only for a moment.

But it's more than that. As I tell the stories, I can't help but think of Lily—of the light she's brought back into my life, of the way she's made me believe in love again. The audience is here for the stories, but in my heart, every word, every shadowed moment, is for her. She's standing at the edge of the crowd, her eyes fixed on me with a look of admiration that makes my heart ache with something close to hope.

The story comes to its climax, and I let my voice drop, drawing out the suspense before delivering the final, chilling twist. There's a collective gasp from the crowd, followed by a moment of stunned silence before the applause breaks out. I take a deep breath, feeling the rush of satisfaction that comes with a story well told. But more than that, I feel something else—a sense of fulfillment, of purpose, that I haven't felt in years.

As the crowd begins to disperse, I catch sight of Lily standing a little apart, her face lit by the soft glow of the lanterns. There's a look in her eyes, something bright and tender, that makes my decision all the more clear. This is the moment. I can't wait any longer.

I make my way over to her, my heart pounding with anticipation and a hint of fear. She smiles as I approach, and it's all I can do to keep my thoughts in order. I don't want to mess this up, but I know that whatever happens next, I have to be honest with her. I have to tell her how I feel.

"Logan, that was amazing," she says softly, her voice full of admiration. "You really have a gift."

"Thanks," I reply, my voice a little rough around the edges. I take a breath, trying to steady myself. "Can we... can we talk for a minute? Somewhere quiet?"

She nods, her eyes searching mine as if she can sense the weight of what I'm about to say. I lead her away from the remaining crowd, to a quiet spot under the trees where the lantern light filters through the branches, casting a warm, golden glow around us. The sounds of the Bash fade into the background, leaving just the two of us in the stillness of the night.

I turn to face her, my heart racing, my hands suddenly feeling too big, too awkward. But when I look into her eyes, all the fear, all the doubt, seems to fade away, replaced by a sense of certainty that I haven't felt in a long time.

"Lily," I begin, my voice low and steady, but filled with the emotion I can no longer hold back. "I need to tell you something. Something I've been wanting to say for a while now."

She watches me, her eyes wide and bright, and I can see the hope there, the anticipation that mirrors my own.

"You've brought something back into my life that I thought I'd lost forever," I continue, my voice growing softer, more vulnerable. "When Emily died, I didn't think I'd ever be able to feel... this way again. I shut myself off, thinking that it was the only way to protect myself. But you... you've changed that. You've brought light back into my life, Lily. You've made me believe in love again."

Her breath catches, and I can see the emotions flickering across her face—surprise, joy, and something deeper, something that makes my heart ache with hope.

"I'm falling in love with you, Lily," I say, the words finally out in the open, filling the space between us. "And I know it's scary, and I know it's risky, but I can't keep it to myself anymore. I don't want to."

For a moment, the world seems to hold its breath, and I can feel my heart pounding in my chest, the vulnerability of the moment almost overwhelming. But then Lily steps closer, her eyes shining with unshed tears, her smile soft and full of emotion.

"Logan," she whispers, her voice trembling with the weight of her feelings. "I've been falling for you too. I was so scared to admit it, scared of what it might mean, but... I love you. I really do."

The relief that washes over me is indescribable, flooding my senses and leaving me momentarily speechless. Before I can fully process the significance of her words, before I can articulate any further thoughts, I instinctively pull her into my arms. She comes willingly, her arms encircling my neck, and I draw her close, savoring the warmth of her body pressed against mine. In that intimate embrace, I can feel the steady beat of her heart echoing my own, a rhythmic reassurance that we are no longer alone in our feelings, and that this moment is ours to cherish.

And then, under the glow of the lanterns, with the magic of the night wrapping around us, I kiss her. It's soft and tender, filled with all the emotions we've been holding back, all the love that's been growing between us. It feels like a promise, a commitment, a new beginning all rolled into one, and as her lips move against mine, I know that this is where I'm meant to be. Here, with her.

When we finally pull back, breathless and a little dazed from the intensity of the moment, I can see the same realization reflected in her bright green eyes, the same certainty illuminating her expression that this is undeniably right, that this is where we're meant to be, together in this shared space where time seems to stand still.

"I love you, Lily," I whisper, my voice barely audible, but filled with the truth of the words. "And I'm not going anywhere."

She smiles, her eyes bright with happiness, and I know that whatever comes next, we'll face it together. Because tonight, everything has changed, and for the first time in a long time, I'm not afraid. I'm ready.

CHAPTER 13

Lily

THE NIGHT AIR IS COOL, tinged with the crispness of autumn, as the soft strains of music fill the town square. Lanterns hang from every tree and lamppost, casting a warm, golden glow over the scene. The stars above twinkle like a thousand tiny lanterns themselves, and the entire town seems to be bathed in a magical light. It's the perfect setting for the Lantern-Lit Dance, a tradition in Buttercup Bay that symbolizes unity and the enduring light of our community.

As I stand on the edge of the square, watching the townspeople pair up and move to the music, I feel a sense of peace settle over me. This is everything I've worked for, everything my grandmother dreamed of for this town—and I'm here, right in the middle of it, feeling like I belong.

And then I see Logan. He's making his way toward me, his gaze fixed on mine, and the rest of the world seems to fade away. There's something in the way he looks at me tonight—something that makes my heart flutter, and my breath catch in my throat. It's a look that says he's here for me, that he's made his choice, and that choice is us.

"Lily," he says softly when he reaches me, holding out his hand. "Will you dance with me?"

There's no hesitation in my answer. "Yes, I'd love to."

He takes my hand, and together we glide into the heart of the square, where the world seems to dissolve around us. The music drifts softly through the air, a lilting melody that envelops us like a warm blanket on a chilly night. Logan pulls me close, his strong arm encircling my waist, and I nestle my head against his chest, letting the comforting rhythm of his heartbeat guide our steps. The sweet notes weave through the atmosphere, making the moment feel both ethereal and beautifully intimate, as if time has paused just for us.

As we sway together under the stars, surrounded by the warm glow of the lanterns, I feel a deep sense of peace settle over me. It's as if the world has finally righted itself, as if everything has fallen into place exactly where it's meant to be. And for the first time, I know without a doubt that this is where I belong—right here, in Logan's arms, in this town that I love.

"I love you, Lily," Logan whispers, his voice barely audible above the music, but filled with a depth of emotion that makes my heart swell. "I want to build a life with you. A future. Together."

His words are like a balm to my soul, soothing all the fears and doubts that have held me back for so long. Tears of joy well up in my eyes, and I look up at him, seeing the vulnerability in his expression, the hope that matches my own.

"I love you too, Logan," I whisper back, my voice thick with emotion. "I want that more than anything. A future with you. I promise."

He smiles, a look of pure happiness on his face, and I know that this is the moment that changes everything. This is the moment when we leave the past behind and step into a future that's bright and full of promise.

As the dance comes to an end, the music fading into the night, the townspeople around us break into applause and cheers. I hadn't even realized they were watching, but now I see their smiles, their approving nods, and it fills me with warmth. They're not just celebrating the Bash—they're celebrating us, our love, and the new beginning we've found together.

The applause fades, and the night is quiet for a moment, the only sound the rustle of leaves in the breeze. Then, with a sudden burst of color, the sky above us lights up with fireworks. The display is spectacular—brilliant reds, blues, and golds exploding in the night sky, casting a shimmering light over the square. The crowd gasps in delight, and I can't help but smile as I watch the display, feeling like the whole world is celebrating with us.

But then Logan turns to me, holding something in his hand, and my attention shifts entirely to him. It's a lantern—handcrafted and beautifully etched with delicate symbols of love, hope, and new beginnings. He holds it out to me, his eyes soft and filled with love.

"This is for you," he says quietly, his voice full of emotion. "It represents our future together—a future that's bright and full of promise. Just like this lantern."

My heart swells with love as I take the lantern from him, my fingers brushing against his. The craftsmanship is exquisite, and I can see the care and thought he's put into every detail. It's more than just a gift—it's a symbol of everything we've been through, everything we've overcome, and everything we have to look forward to.

"Thank you, Logan," I say, my voice barely more than a whisper. "It's beautiful."

He smiles, his eyes shining with emotion, and then he leans in, pressing his lips to mine in a tender, heartfelt kiss. It's soft and sweet, filled with all the love and promise that we've been building between us, and as the fireworks burst overhead, I feel like the world has finally aligned in the way it was always meant to.

When we pull back, we're both breathless, a little dazed by the intensity of the moment. But there's a certainty in Logan's eyes that mirrors my own, a sense of knowing that this is where we're meant to be—together, in this moment, with a future that's as bright and beautiful as the lantern he's given me.

"I'm ready," I whisper, holding his gaze, letting him see the truth in my words. "I'm ready for whatever comes next, as long as it's with you."

"So am I," he replies, his voice full of conviction. "And I promise you, Lily, it's going to be amazing."

We stand there for a moment longer, holding each other close, watching the fireworks light up the sky. The world around us seems to fade away, leaving just the two of us, surrounded by the warmth of the lanterns and the love that's grown between us. And in that moment, I know that we're ready—ready to leave the past behind, ready to embrace the future, and ready to build a life together that's filled with love, hope, and new beginnings.

CHAPTER 14

Logan

THE MORNING AIR is crisp and clear, carrying the faint scent of pine and the lingering sweetness of last night's celebration. I sit on the porch of the Buttercup Inn, a mug of steaming coffee in my hands, watching as the town of Buttercup Bay slowly comes to life. The streets are quiet, still wrapped in the afterglow of the Halloween Bash, but there's a sense of contentment in the air, a shared satisfaction in what we all accomplished together.

Beside me, Lily sits with her own mug, her legs tucked up beneath her as she leans against the porch railing. Her auburn hair catches the early morning light, and I can see the peace in her expression, the way her shoulders have relaxed now that the weight of the Bash has finally lifted. We've been sitting here in comfortable silence for a while, just soaking in the moment, but I can feel the warmth of her presence beside me, grounding me in a way I never thought possible.

Last night was perfect. The Bash was everything Lily dreamed it would be and more. The town came together in a way that reminded me why I fell in love with this place—and with her. As I sit here now, reflecting on everything that's happened, there's a deep sense of peace that settles over me, a contentment that comes from knowing I've made the right decision in opening my heart again.

I glance over at Lily, taking in the way her eyes sparkle as she gazes out at the town, the soft smile playing on her lips. She turns to me, catching my eye, and her smile widens, filling me with a warmth that I've come to cherish.

"Last night was amazing," she says softly, her voice carrying the contentment I feel. "I still can't believe it all came together so perfectly."

"It was all because of you," I reply, my voice just as soft. "You made it happen, Lily."

She shakes her head, a modest laugh escaping her lips. "*We* made it happen. I couldn't have done it without you."

I reach over, taking her hand in mine, and she squeezes it gently, her touch a reassurance that we're in this together. "I'm glad I was here," I say, the words filled with more meaning than just last night's event. "I'm glad we're doing this together."

We fall into a comfortable silence again, but this time, it's filled with the promise of what's to come. There's no rush, no need to fill the space with words, because we both know where we stand—side by side, ready to take on whatever comes next.

The town is beginning to wake up now, the first signs of life appearing in the streets as people start their day. I can see Greg opening up his bakery across the square, the scent of fresh bread wafting through the air, and Mrs. Whittaker bustling down the street, no doubt heading for her usual morning coffee. It's a scene that's become familiar to me over the past few weeks, but today, it feels different. Today, it feels like home.

As I take another sip of my coffee, I think about the changes that are coming—moving into town, merging my life with Lily's, becoming a part of this community in a way I never expected. It's a big step, but it's one I'm ready for. My cabin in the woods will always be a retreat, a place where Lily and I can escape when we need to, but our home... our home is here, in the heart of Buttercup Bay.

"I was thinking," I say, breaking the silence. "Maybe we could start planning some renovations for the Inn. Make it more... you."

Lily turns to me, her eyes lighting up with excitement. "I'd love that. There's so much I've thought about doing since I took over."

"We could add a bigger kitchen," I suggest, my mind already spinning with possibilities. "Maybe even a workshop for me to keep up with my woodworking."

"And a new garden," she adds, her enthusiasm contagious. "With space for all the flowers and herbs I've been dreaming of planting."

I smile, imagining the life we're about to build together, the home we're going to create. "It's going to be perfect, Lily."

She nods, her eyes shining with joy. "It already is."

As we sit there, making plans for our future, I can feel the last remnants of fear and doubt slipping away. The love and support of this community, the acceptance I've found here, and most importantly, the love I share with Lily—these are the things that have replaced the loneliness and uncertainty that once held me back.

As I watch the town gradually come to life in the soft morning light, I feel a profound sense of belonging wash over me, as if I have finally discovered my true place in the world. The fear that once kept me isolated and alone has been completely transformed, now replaced by the unwavering love and support of this vibrant community, along with the deep, abiding love I share with Lily. Her presence in my life has anchored me in ways I never thought possible. And in this moment, I know, without a shadow of a doubt, that this is precisely where I'm meant to be, surrounded by familiar faces and the warmth of a home that feels like it was always waiting for me.

Lily squeezes my hand again, her touch a gentle reminder that I am anchored in this moment. She pulls me from my thoughts, and I can't help but focus on her radiant smile. "You know," she says, her voice soft and full of warmth, like a comforting embrace, "I think this is just the beginning. There's so much more we're going to do, so much more we're going to build together." Her words dance in the air between us, brimming with possibility and hope, igniting a spark of excitement deep within me.

I turn to her, my heart full to bursting. "I can't wait," I reply, my voice steady and sure. "Whatever comes next, I'm ready for it. As long as we're together."

She smiles, her eyes bright with love, and in that moment, I know that everything I've been through, every choice I've made, has led me to this. To her. To this life we're about to build together.

And as the sun rises higher in the sky, casting its golden light over the town, I feel a deep sense of peace settle over me. I'm home. I'm where I'm meant to be.

CHAPTER 15

Lily

THE MORNING SUN filters through the windows of the Buttercup Inn, casting a warm, golden light across the room. I'm sitting at the kitchen table with Logan, a blueprint of the inn spread out between us, the smell of freshly brewed coffee filling the air. It's a simple moment, but it feels monumental—like the beginning of something new and beautiful.

We've been talking about renovations for the inn, the changes we want to make to create a space that's truly ours. The Buttercup Inn has always been a symbol of my grandmother's legacy, a place that embodies the heart and soul of Buttercup Bay. But now, as Logan and I plan our future together, it's becoming something more—a reflection of our love, of the life we're building together.

"I was thinking," Logan says, his voice thoughtful as he studies the blueprint, "we could open up the kitchen a bit, make it more spacious. Maybe add a big farmhouse table where we can host dinners for the community."

I smile at the thought, picturing the warmth and laughter that would fill the inn during those gatherings. "I love that idea. It would make the inn feel even more like home."

Logan looks up at me, his blue eyes filled with warmth. "That's what I want, Lily. I want this place to be our home—a place where we can create new memories and traditions, while still honoring the past."

His words touch something deep inside me, and I reach across the table to take his hand, feeling the steady strength in his grip. "It already feels like home," I say softly, my heart swelling with love and contentment. "Because you're here."

We sit like that for a moment, just holding hands, the blueprint between us a symbol of everything we're about to build together. I've never felt more certain of anything in my life. Logan and I are exactly where we're meant to be—planning a future that's bright and full of promise.

Later that day, we gather with a small group of friends and townspeople at the Hollow Inn. It's a cozy gathering, the inn filled with the sound of laughter and conversation. The sunlight streams in through the windows, casting a warm glow over the room, and there's a sense of joy in the air, a feeling that something special is about to happen.

Logan and I stand together at the front of the room, my hand in his, and I feel a rush of excitement as we prepare to share our news. I glance up at him, seeing the love and pride in his eyes, and it gives me the courage I need to speak.

"We wanted to thank all of you for being here today," I begin, my voice strong and steady despite the butterflies in my stomach. "This community has been such a big part of our lives, and we're so grateful for your support."

I pause, feeling the anticipation in the room, and then I smile, unable to contain my excitement any longer. "Logan and I have some news to share. We're engaged!"

There's a moment of stunned silence, and then the room erupts into cheers and applause. I can see the joy on everyone's faces, the way they're beaming with happiness for us, and it fills me with a deep sense of belonging. This isn't just a town—it's a family. And they're welcoming Logan and me with open arms.

"And that's not all," Logan adds, his voice filled with the same excitement I feel. "We're planning a Halloween-themed wedding next year, right here in Buttercup Bay. We can't imagine a more perfect place to start our life together."

The cheers grow louder, and I can see people exchanging excited looks, already imagining what our wedding will be like. The sense of community is overwhelming, and I feel tears prickling at the corners of my eyes as I look around the room, taking in the love and support that surrounds us.

As the excitement begins to settle, Logan and I move through the room, accepting hugs and congratulations from our friends. Mrs. Whittaker, who's been one of my biggest supporters since the Bash, pulls me into a tight embrace, her eyes shining with happiness.

"I knew it," she says with a grin. "I knew the two of you were meant to be together. Your grandmother would be so proud, Lily."

Her heartfelt words bring a sudden lump to my throat, and I fight to blink back tears as I look at her, my smile genuine and warm. "Thank you, Mrs. Whittaker. That means so much to me," I reply, my voice slightly shaky with emotion, the weight of her support wrapping around me like a comforting blanket.

She pats my hand affectionately. "You've done well, my dear. I can't wait to see what the future holds for you both."

The rest of the afternoon passes in a blur of joy and celebration, the inn filled with laughter and the warmth of friendship. But as the sun begins to set, casting a golden light over the town, Logan and I find a quiet moment together on the porch, away from the bustle of the gathering.

We sit side by side, holding hands, watching as the sky turns shades of pink and orange. It's a beautiful, peaceful moment, and I feel a deep sense of contentment as I lean my head on Logan's shoulder, letting the warmth of his presence surround me.

"I can't believe how far we've come," I say softly, my voice filled with wonder. "It feels like just yesterday we were strangers, and now... now we're planning a life together."

Logan turns his head, pressing a kiss to the top of my head. "It's been an incredible journey, Lily. And it's only just beginning. We have so much to look forward to."

A smile spreads across my face, my heart swelling with an overwhelming love for the man who has become my everything. "I know," I reply, feeling the warmth of his affection seep deeper into my soul. "And I can't wait to see where this incredible journey takes us, hand in hand, creating memories that will last a lifetime."

We sit there for a while longer, watching as the sun dips below the horizon, the sky fading into twilight. The world around us is quiet, the town settling into the calm of the evening, and it feels like the perfect ending to a perfect day.

As the first stars begin to twinkle in the deepening indigo sky, Logan gently squeezes my hand, his voice soft and filled with a warmth that sends shivers down my spine. "We have a lifetime of happiness ahead of us, Lily. And I promise you, I'll be by your side through it all, no matter the challenges we may face or the dreams we dare to chase." His words hang in the air, wrapping around us like a comforting blanket, and I find myself lost in the depths of his gaze, filled with unwavering devotion.

I look up at him, my eyes shining with tears of joy. "I know, Logan. And I'll be by yours. Always."

We share a tender kiss, the promise of our future sealed in that moment. As we pull back, I rest my head against his shoulder once more, feeling the steady beat of his heart beneath my cheek.

This is where I'm meant to be. With Logan, in this town, building a life together that's filled with love, hope, and the promise of new beginnings. And I know, deep in my heart, that our love is strong enough to weather any storm.

As we sit there in the quiet of the evening, I close my eyes, feeling a deep sense of peace settle over me. This is our new beginning, and I'm ready for whatever the future holds.

CHAPTER 16

Lily

THE TOWN SQUARE is a scene straight out of a fairytale. Lanterns hang from every tree, their soft glow casting warm, golden light across the square. Pumpkins of all shapes and sizes line the paths, their carved faces flickering with the light of the candles inside. Autumn leaves, in shades of red, orange, and gold, create a vibrant carpet underfoot, and the air is filled with the crisp scent of the season. It's everything I ever dreamed of—and more.

Today is our wedding day.

I stand at the edge of the square, taking it all in—the decorations, the townspeople, the joy that fills the air—and my heart swells with emotion. This is the place where our story began, where Logan and I found each other, and where we've chosen to start our new life together. The magic of Buttercup Bay is all around us, wrapping us in its warm embrace, and I can't imagine a more perfect setting for this moment.

The ceremony is about to begin, and I can feel the anticipation buzzing in the air. Friends, family, and townspeople have gathered to celebrate with us, their faces filled with love and happiness. As I step forward, I catch sight of Logan standing at the front of the square, waiting for me. Our eyes meet, and the world seems to fall away, leaving just the two of us.

Logan looks more handsome than ever, his dark hair slightly tousled by the breeze, his blue eyes filled with the same love and devotion that I feel in my own heart. He smiles as I approach, and the warmth in his gaze makes me feel like I'm walking on air.

When I reach him, he takes my hand in his, and the touch of his skin against mine grounds me, reminding me that this is real—this is happening. We're about to exchange vows, to commit our lives to each other, surrounded by the people who have become our family.

The officiant begins the ceremony, his voice steady and warm as he speaks of love, commitment, and the journey that has brought us to this moment. As I stand there, holding Logan's hand, I feel a deep sense of peace settle over me. This is where I'm meant to be—right here, with Logan, in the heart of Buttercup Bay.

When it's time to exchange vows, Logan turns to me, his voice filled with emotion as he speaks. "Lily, from the moment I met you, my life changed in ways I never imagined. You've brought light back into my world, made me believe in love again, and given me a reason to hope for the future. Today, I promise to stand by your side, to love you with all that I am, and to build a life together that honors the past while embracing the future. I love you, now and always."

Tears well up in my eyes as I listen to his words, the depth of his love wrapping around me like a warm blanket. When it's my turn, my voice trembles with emotion, but there's no doubt in my heart. "Logan, you've shown me what it means to be truly loved. You've given me a home in your heart and a future that's bright and full of promise. Today, I vow to love you, to cherish you, and to walk with you through all of life's adventures. Together, we will create new traditions, build a life filled with love, and hold onto the magic that first brought us together. I love you, now and forever."

As I finish speaking, I see the emotion in Logan's eyes, and I know that we're not just making a promise to each other—we're creating a legacy, a love story that will become a cherished part of Buttercup Bay's lore. It's a story of unexpected, enchanting love, one that will inspire others to believe in the power of magic and hope.

When the officiant finally pronounces us husband and wife, a joyous cheer erupts from the crowd, echoing off the walls of Buttercup Bay, and in that moment, I feel an overwhelming swell of emotion, as if my heart might burst from the sheer happiness enveloping me. Logan leans in closer, our eyes locking in a shared understanding of this monumental moment, and our first kiss as a married couple is soft and tender, a sweet union filled with the promise of countless adventures and a lifetime of unwavering love.

The celebration that follows is a breathtaking blur of joy and laughter, a vivid tapestry of emotions woven together in a tapestry of happiness. The town square has been transformed into a dazzling wonderland of light and color, where strings of twinkling lights cascade from the trees like stars come to life. Tables overflow with an array of delicious food, each dish more tempting than the last, while the lively music fills the air, infusing it with an infectious festive spirit. Everywhere I turn, I see the warm, familiar faces of people I love—smiling, laughing, and celebrating alongside us, their joy radiating like the lights that illuminate the night. Each heartfelt cheer and gentle embrace wraps around me, making me feel as though I am floating on clouds of euphoria in this magical moment.

As the evening deepens, the lanterns glow brighter, casting a magical light over the square. Logan and I move to the center, where the music shifts to a slower, more intimate melody. He takes me in his arms, and we begin to dance, our movements slow and graceful, as if the world has faded away and left just the two of us.

The stars twinkle above, and the lanterns sway gently in the breeze, creating a scene that feels almost too perfect to be real. But it is real—this is our life, our love, and the future we've chosen to build together.

As we dance, Logan leans down, his voice a soft whisper in my ear. "I love you, Lily. Today, tomorrow, and always."

I look up at him, my heart full to bursting. "I love you too, Logan. More than words can say."

We continue to dance, our steps in perfect harmony, and I know that this moment is the culmination of everything we've been through—the doubts, the fears, the joys, and the love. It's all led us here to this magical night under the stars.

When the music ends, the applause of our friends and family surrounds us, but in my heart, there's only Logan. We share another kiss, sealing the promise we've made to each other, and I know that our love will only grow stronger with each passing day.

As the celebration winds down, Logan and I take a leisurely walk through the charming town, hand in hand, our fingers intertwined like the threads of our lives. The streets are quiet now, the laughter and music fading into the background, leaving only the gentle rustle of leaves and the distant sound of a night owl. The lanterns cast a soft, golden glow on the cobblestones, illuminating our path and creating a romantic atmosphere that feels almost enchanted. The night air is cool and refreshing, wrapping around us like a comforting embrace, carrying with it the sweet scent of blooming jasmine from nearby gardens. It feels like the perfect end to a perfect day, a moment suspended in time where nothing else matters but us and the love that has blossomed between us.

"This is where it all began," I say softly, as we pass by the town square, now empty and peaceful. "I can't believe how much has changed."

Logan squeezes my hand, his grip steady and reassuring. "And yet, in so many ways, it feels like everything is exactly as it should be. We're exactly where we're meant to be."

I smile, knowing he's right. This town, this community, this love—it's all part of our story, a story that's just beginning. As we walk together, the future stretching out before us, I know that whatever comes next, we'll face it together, hand in hand.

We reach the Buttercup Inn, our home, and I feel a sense of peace settle over me. Logan opens the door, and we step inside, the warmth of the inn wrapping around us like a welcome embrace.

As we close the door behind us, leaving the world outside, I know that this is just the beginning of a new chapter in our lives—a chapter filled with love, happiness, and the magic of Buttercup Bay. And as long as we're together, I know that our love will light the way, guiding us through whatever the future holds.

Leave a review!

If you enjoyed this book, take a moment to leave a
review. This allows your fellow readers to determine
if this is a good book for them.

Thank you!